STORIES IN A SEASHELL

by Alex Nogués Otero
illustrated by Silvia Cabestany

StarBerry Books
New York

Publisher's Cataloging-in-Publication Data
Names: Nogués Otero, Alex, author. | Cabestany, Silvia, illustrator.
Title: Stories in a seashell / by Alex Nogués Otero ; illustrated by Silvia Cabestany.
Description: New York, NY: StarBerry Books, an imprint of Kane Press, Inc., 2018.
Identifiers: ISBN 9781575659688 (Hardcover) | 9781575659695 (ebook) | LCCN 2017953522
Summary: A child holds a seashell up to his ear and hears mermaids, fishermen, whales, submarines, and other sounds of the sea inside.
Subjects: LCSH Marine animals--Juvenile fiction. | Seashells--Juvenile fiction. | Imagination--Juvenile fiction. | Sea stories. | BISAC JUVENILE FICTION / Imagination & Play | JUVENILE FICTION / Animals / Marine Life | JUVENILE FICTION / Action & Adventure / General
Classification: LCC PZ7.N67196 St 2018 | DDC [E]--dc23

Library of Congress Control Number: 2017953522

10 9 8 7 6 5 4 3 2 1

First published in English in the United States of America in 2018
by StarBerry Books, an imprint of Kane Press, Inc.
Printed in China

StarBerry Books is a trademark of Kane Press, Inc.

Visit us online at www.kanepress.com

 Like us on Facebook
facebook.com/kanepress

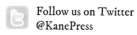 Follow us on Twitter
@KanePress

STORIES IN A SEASHELL

Max was strolling around the beach picking up shells,
scaring away crabs, and looking at his footprints
disappearing under the waves.

He found a shell near the seashore.
He picked it up and held it close to his ear
to see if it was true that one could hear the sea inside.

And he heard it perfectly. He heard the waves and the wind.
The cawing of seagulls.

He heard a pirate ship plowing through the sea.
And he heard, from the highest mast, the voice
of the lookout who was announcing . . .

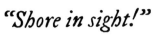

"Shore in sight!"

The shore belonged to a tiny island,

where one could hear a stranded sailor
shouting, *"Help!"*

Not far away, a young mermaid heard the
shout and swam off to the rescue. . . .

"Shiver me timbers!"

An old fisherman and his cabin boy were
amazed at the sight of the mermaid
who had just passed by. . . .

They didn't see the storm that was approaching.
Baroouuummmmm.
Thunder broke
through the sky.

Whoooooooooshh.
Rain flooded the sea.

On the coast,
waves were breaking on the cliffs.
Splassshhh, it echoed in Max's shell.

And Max could hear the calls of puffins
coming from high above.
One of them swooped down and he heard
the flapping of its wings.

The puffin landed on the mast of a boat moored on a quiet beach.
The sea was pulling away the stones on the beach
and it made a little noise, like tickling.

Sitting on the beach,
a poet was gazing toward the sun.
In the shell, Max could hear a sigh . . .

... and then a strong *puff*.
The enormous back of a dark gray whale emerged
from the sea and blocked the poet's view of the sun.

The whale spit gallons and gallons of steam
and afterwards, with a great crash,
plunged down deep.

There,
circled by millions of silent jellyfish,
the whale sang its melodic song
hoping to find its family. . . .

Many miles away,
a submarine's radio picked up
the song of the whale.

The submarine captain heard the sound
and thought he had been sighted.
Max heard the alarms and the engines of
the submarine. The captain stroked his
mustache and activated the periscope. . . .

He saw a beach.

And on the beach, a little boy.

A little boy who was holding a big shell against his ear and who'd heard people say the sea lived inside it.